Chasing Degas

Abrams Books for Young Readers
New York

Eva Montanari

*I*t was our last rehearsal before the recital. We'd practiced the ballet so many times that I could dance it in my sleep.

In my bag I had packed my new tutu. I couldn't wait to wear it on my big night!

Monsieur Degas had just left the opera house. He was an artist who often painted the ballet students while we practiced. I ran to his easel to see what he had worked on. He had painted me right in the foreground . . . while I was scratching my back! I was so embarrassed.

I went to my bag so that I could try on the tutu, but when I opened it, I found a big surprise—it was full of Monsieur Degas' paints! We must have accidentally taken each other's bag.

I rushed out of the opera house and into the pouring rain. I had to find Monsieur Degas before the performance!

I stopped under an awning to shield myself from the rain.

There, I saw another painter.

"Excuse me, but have you seen Monsieur Degas?" I asked.

"He is a painter, too."

"Oh yes, I know Monsieur Degas. But I haven't seen him today," the man answered. "I've been very busy painting this street, trying to capture this moment before the rain stops."

"I must find Monsieur Degas right away," I said.

"Perhaps my friend who is staying in that hotel room up there has seen him. He has very sharp eyes and never misses anything." He shouted up to the window, "Monsieur Monet, can you help this little ballerina?"

Monsieur Monet put his head out the window. "What did you say, Monsieur Caillebotte?"

"Have you seen Monsieur Degas?" Monsieur Caillebotte asked.

Monsieur Monet pointed at a dot on his canvas. "But of course!" he said. "He's right here. I saw him walking down the boulevard and added him to my painting. But he isn't at the end of the street now, because time passes."

"Do you know where he was going?" I asked.

"Why don't you go to the Moulin de la Galette," he said. "Perhaps he went for some lunch." Monsieur Monet replaced the canvas on his easel. "The rain has stopped and the light has changed—I must start a new painting!"

"Thank you, Monsieur Monet and Monsieur Caillebotte," I said as I continued on.

The sun was shining when I reached the Moulin de la Galette. There, I saw a man painting on a large canvas, and beside him was Monsieur Degas!

People were dancing all around the café. All I needed to do was cross the dance floor to reach him, but soon I was doing a pirouette. A man even lifted me into the air!

By the time I finally reached the other side, Monsieur Degas was gone!

"Hello, mademoiselle," the painter said as he looked over his easel. "I am Monsieur Renoir. How can I help you?"

I watched as Monsieur Renoir painted the dancing crowd behind me with short brushstrokes of pure color.

"Do you know where I can find Monsieur Degas?" I asked.

"He went to Père Tanguy's shop to buy more paint," he said.

"Paint?!" I laughed and showed him what was in my bag.

Monsieur Renoir didn't laugh.

He took out the tube of black paint and said very seriously, "Did you know that the color black doesn't exist in nature?"

"Then what color is my hair?" I asked.

Monsieur Renoir pulled out the other tubes of paint. "Your hair is a touch of red and brown and, yes, a little bit of green," he said.

"Green!" I exclaimed.

"Yes. I would use all these colors if I were to paint your beautiful hair," he said.

I looked closer at Monsieur Renoir's painting and noticed how he used many colors in order to capture each detail.

"If you want to see more paints, you should visit Père Tanguy," Monsieur Renoir said. "He owns the best paint store in Paris. Perhaps he knows where Monsieur Degas is."

"I must go now if I'm going to catch up with Monsieur Degas!"

I rushed to the paint store, where I found
Père Tanguy.

"Is Monsieur Degas still here?" I asked.

"Degas," he said with a sigh. "He is the only painter who pays me for paint. Did you know that all the other painters who come to my store pay me with paintings?"

I looked at the stacks of paintings in his store.

"Sisley, Monet, Morisot, Pissaro . . . I have many of their original paintings here. Even one painted by Mary Cassatt. She is an American woman who paints in Paris."

"A lady who paints?" I asked.

"Yes. Monsieur Degas just left to take her a tube of turquoise. If you hurry, perhaps you can still find him at her studio," he said.

"Thank you for your help, Père Tanguy," I said. And again, I ran off.

When I reached the studio of Mary Cassatt, a young girl like me answered the door.

"Are you Mary Cassatt?" I asked.

"No, I'm one of her models," the girl replied. "Come right this way."

Once in the sitting room, the model plopped back down lazily in a big blue chair, where a woman continued to paint her. Mary Cassatt used the most beautiful shades of blue.

"Pardon me, Madame Cassatt, but is Monsieur Degas still here?" I asked.

"You just missed him!" she answered. "He was off to the opera house to paint tonight's performance."

"I must find him first!" I cried. I thanked Mary Cassatt and the girl and continued the hunt for Monsieur Degas. Time was running out!

I ran
through the
streets of Paris
and started across the
bridge to the opera house. At
the end of the bridge, I could see
a man wearing a tall hat—at last, it was
Monsieur Degas!"

I rushed toward him. "Monsieur Degas?" I asked
shyly.

"So this must be your tutu," he said as he handed
me my bag. "You must have been looking
everywhere for it."

"Thank you, Monsieur Degas," I said. "I have searched all over the city for you. Here are your paints."

"Many thanks to you, mademoiselle," he said. "Without these paints, I wouldn't be able to paint the recital tonight."

Together we walked to the opera house. I told Monsieur Degas about all I had seen and learned that day. I told him about meeting Monsieur Caillebotte, Monsieur Monet, Monsieur Renoir, Père Tanguy, and Mary Cassatt.

We arrived at the opera house and said good-bye. I rushed backstage and changed into my tutu without even looking in the mirror. Monsieur Degas went to set up his easel.

The orchestra began to play, and I leaped onto the stage!

I turned and twirled and jumped. I danced for all the special painters I had met that day, but most of all, I danced for my new friend, Monsieur Degas.

After the recital, Monsieur Degas came backstage. He showed
me the painting he had begun.

"It's me!" I exclaimed.

"You certainly were the star of the show tonight," Monsieur
Degas said. Then he handed me his bag of paints. "After today,
I think these should belong to you."

I took the brush and started to swirl and sway. And I watched
as the colors danced and pirouetted around me.

The original paintings that inspired
Chasing Degas

Edgar Degas, French (1834–1917). *The Dance Class*, 1873–1876.
Oil on canvas, 33 ²/₅ x 29 ¹/₂ inches (85 x 75 cm).
Musée d'Orsay, Paris, France
RF 1976
Photograph by Hervé Lewandowski
Photography © Réunion des Musées Nationaux / Art Resource, NY

Claude Monet, French (1840–1926). *Boulevard des Capucines*,
    1873–1874.
Oil on canvas, 31 ⁵/₈ x 23 ³/4 inches (80.3 x 60.3 cm).
The Nelson-Atkins Museum of Art, Kansas City, Missouri
Purchase: The Kenneth A. and Helen F. Spencer Foundation Acquisition
    Fund, F72-35
Photograph by Jamison Miller

Gustave Caillebotte, French (1848–1894). *Paris Street; Rainy Day*,
    1877.
Oil on canvas, 83 ¹/₂ x 108 ³/4 inches (212.2 x 276.2 cm).
The Art Institute of Chicago, Chicago, Illinois
Charles H. and Mary F. S. Worcester Collection, 1964.336
Photography © The Art Institute of Chicago

Auguste Renoir, French (1841–1919). *Bal du Moulin de la Galette,
    Montmartre*, 1876.
Oil on canvas, 51 ¹/₂ x 68 ⁹/10 inches (131 x 175 cm).
Musée d'Orsay, Paris, France
RF 2739
Photograph by Hervé Lewandowski
Photography © Réunion des Musées Nationaux / Art Resource, NY

Mary Cassatt, American (1844–1926). *Little Girl in a Blue Armchair*, 1878.
Oil on canvas, 35 1/4 x 51 1/8 inches (89.5 x 129.8 cm).
National Gallery of Art, Washington
Collection of Mr. and Mrs. Paul Mellon, 1983.1.1.18
Image courtesy of the Board of Trustees, National Gallery of Art, Washington

Edgar Degas, French (1834–1917). *Ballet; L'étoile*, c. 1876–1877.
Pastel over monotype, 22 5/8 x 16 1/2 inches (58 x 42 cm).
Musée d'Orsay, Paris, France
RF 12258
Photograph by J. Schormans
Photography © Réunion des Musées Nationaux / Art Resource, NY

Impressionism was a style of painting that started in Paris, France, around 1860. The Impressionist art movement lasted about forty years, during which time a small group of artists lived, painted, and exhibited in and around Paris.

The Impressionist painters wanted to capture the fleeting moments of contemporary, everyday life. They were especially interested in light and how it moved and changed throughout the day. Using short, thick brushstrokes to show movement, they tried to re-create how it felt to look at the scenes they were painting. They wanted the viewer to see through their eyes. They mixed their colors very sparingly, believing that pure colors applied side by side would better create the vibrations that colors give off in real life. Black was thought of as the absence of color and light, and was therefore avoided by most Impressionists (although Degas did use it!).

Impressionism was not very well liked at first. In fact, it got its name from a bad review of the group's first show in 1874! A critic said that all the paintings looked unfinished. In poking fun at Monet's painting *Impression, Sunrise*, he said that the paintings in the show looked like only "impressions" of finished paintings.

Members of the group came and went, but the main artists of the Impressionist movement are mentioned in *Chasing Degas*: Edgar Degas (1834–1917), Gustave Caillebotte (1848–1894), Claude Monet (1840–1926), Auguste Renoir (1841–1919), Alfred Sisley (1839–99), Camille Pissaro (1830–1903), Berthe Morisot (1841–95), and Mary Cassatt (1844–1926).

Library of Congress Cataloging-in-Publication Data

Montanari, Eva, 1977–
Chasing Degas / by Eva Montanari.
p. cm.
Summary: At the time of the Impressionists, a young ballet
dancer races around Paris, searching for Monsieur Degas,
who accidentally took her bag—and the tutu she needs for
the recital in which she is to perform that night. Includes
reproductions of paintings by French Impressionist
painters, with an author's note.
ISBN 978-0-8109-3878-6
[1. Artists—Fiction. 2. Impressionism (Art)—Fiction.
3. Degas, Edgar, 1834–1917—Fiction. 4. Painting,
French—Fiction. 5. Ballet dancing—Fiction. 6. Paris
(France)—History—1870–1940—Fiction. 7. France—
History—Third Republic, 1870–1940—Fiction.] I.
Title.

PZ7.M76344Ch 2009
[E]—dc22
2008046183

This chase did not really happen, but it could
have! All of the paintings that inspired *Chasing
Degas* were painted within five years of each
other (1873–78) in northern Paris, not far
from the opera house.

❧

Acknowledgments

I would like to thank all the people at Studio
Goodwin Sturges for always believing and
supporting my stories, and especially Judy Sue,
April, and Alison for their infinite patience and
constructive criticism during the whole process
of this book.

❧

To Gabriella Torrini, the first person
to put me on Degas' trail

Text and illustrations copyright © 2009 Eva Montanari
Book design by Maria T. Middleton

Printed and bound in U. S. A.
10 9 8 7 6 5 4 3 2

Abrams Books for Young Readers are available at special
discounts when purchased in quantity for premiums and
promotions as well as fundraising or educational use.
Special editions can also be created to specification. For
details, contact specialmarkets@hnabooks.com or the
address below.

115 West 18th Street
New York, NY 10011
www.abramsbooks.com